Chef

Copyright © QED Publishing 2009

First published in the UK in 2009 by
QED Publishing
A Quarto Group company
226 City Road
London EC1V 2TT
www.qed-publishing.co.uk

A catalogue record for this book is available from
the British Library.

ISBN 978 1 84835 154 7

Printed and bound in China

Author Amanda Askew
Designer and Illustrator Andrew Crowson
Consultants Shirley Bickler and Tracey Dils

Publisher Steve Evans
Creative Director Zeta Davies
Managing Editor Amanda Askew

Words in **bold** are
explained in the
glossary on page 24.

People who help us

Chef

Amanda Askew
Andrew Crowson

QED Publishing

Meet Rory. He's a chef. He cooks food for people at Rory's Diner.

Rory arrives at the **restaurant** at 9 o'clock. The kitchen workers are there to help him to **prepare** the food for lunch.

First, Rory goes over the menu.

"Today, we'll cook leek and potato soup, lamb chops with mint gravy, and chocolate fudge cake."

"Josh, chop the vegetables for the soup. Alice, mix the chocolate cake. Greg, prepare the mint gravy and the mashed potato swirls."

Josh, Greg and Alice start working.

Alice gets the 'Chocolate Delight' recipe book.

Josh starts to chop the leeks and peel the potatoes.

9

Greg picks fresh mint from the **herb** garden.

Alice starts to collect her ingredients.

"Oh no! The fridge has broken down! All the food is ruined!" she shouts.

Rory rushes over to the fridge.

The milk, butter and cheese can't be used. The stock for the gravy will have to be thrown away. The lamb chops will have to be replaced.

Rory phones Farmer John. "We've got an emergency. The fridge is broken. We need milk, butter, cheese and lamb chops – they were today's special."

"I have everything, except lamb chops. Will chicken be ok?"

"Yes, that's fine. I'll serve chicken with mushrooms instead," says Rory.

Farmer John delivers
the new food.

Rory and the team work hard to get everything ready for lunchtime.

People start to arrive
at the restaurant at
12 o'clock.

"Three chicken dishes to table 5 please, Freda," Rory says.

By 2 o'clock, most people are eating their desserts. Rory goes into the **dining area** to meet some of the customers. He likes to see that everyone is happy with their food.

"That was the tastiest chicken I've ever eaten. Thank you very much!" one man tells Rory.

"I'm glad to hear it!" Rory smiles.

Glossary

Dining area A place where people eat food at a table.

Herb A small plant that can be added to food.

Ingredient One of the foods that is used to make a meal.

Menu A list of meals served in a restaurant.

Recipe A list telling you how to cook a meal or type of food.

Restaurant A place where you can buy and eat a meal cooked by a chef.

Prepare To get something ready or make something.